IN SPACE

by Belén Garrido
illustrated by Judy Stead

 Harcourt

Orlando   Boston   Dallas   Chicago   San Diego

Visit *The Learning Site!*
www.harcourtschool.com

Judd runs and jumps.
"Your hat is in the
mud!" says Meg.

2

She gives it to him.
"The sun is out!" says
Judd.

"Meg, look at the pup!
Here comes a bus!"
he says.
4

"Look up!" says Judd.
People look up to see
a blimp.

When night comes,
new surprises are out!

"A big cup!" says Meg.
"A man that hunts!"
says Judd.

Day and night, it's fun
to see what is in
space!